D1168224

## ABOUT THE BANK STREET READY-TO-READ SERIES

More than seventy-five years of educational research, innovative teaching, and quality publishing have earned The Bank Street College of Education its reputation as America's most trusted name in early childhood education.

Because no two children are exactly alike in their development, the Bank Street Ready-to-Read series is written on three levels to accommodate the individual stages of reading readiness of children ages three through eight.

○ *Level 1:* **GETTING READY TO READ (Pre-K–Grade 1)**
Level 1 books are perfect for reading aloud with children who are getting ready to read or just starting to read words or phrases. These books feature large type, repetition, and simple sentences.

● *Level 2:* **READING TOGETHER (Grades 1–3)**
These books have slightly smaller type and longer sentences. They are ideal for children beginning to read by themselves who may need help.

○ *Level 3:* **I CAN READ IT MYSELF (Grades 2–3)**
These stories are just right for children who can read independently. They offer more complex and challenging stories and sentences.

All three levels of The Bank Street Ready-to-Read books make it easy to select the books most appropriate for your child's development and enable him or her to grow with the series step by step. The levels purposely overlap to reinforce skills and further encourage reading.

We feel that making reading fun is the single most important thing anyone can do to help children become good readers. We hope you will become part of Bank Street's long tradition of learning through sharing.

The Bank Street College of Education

For a free color catalog describing Gareth Stevens' list of high-quality books and
multimedia programs, call 1-800-542-2595 (USA) or 1-800-461-9120 (Canada).
Gareth Stevens Publishing's Fax: (414) 225-0377.
See our catalog, too, on the World Wide Web: http://gsinc.com

Library of Congress Cataloging-in-Publication Data

Oppenheim, Joanne.
    "Not now!" said the cow / by Joanne Oppenheim; illustrated by
Chris Demarest.
       p. cm. -- (Bank Street ready-to-read)
    Summary: In this story based on "The Little Red Hen," a little black
crow asks his animal friends to help with the planting of some corn seed.
    ISBN 0-8368-1752-4 (lib. bdg.)
    [1. Folklore.] I. Demarest, Chris L., ill. II. Title. III. Series.
PZ8.1.O57No  1997
398.2'4528617--dc21
    [E]                                                    97-2144

This edition first published in 1997 by
**Gareth Stevens Publishing**
1555 North RiverCenter Drive, Suite 201
Milwaukee, Wisconsin 53212 USA

Printed in Mexico

1 2 3 4 5 6 7 8 9 01 00 99 98 97

Bank Street Ready-to-Read™

# "Not Now!" Said the Cow

by Joanne Oppenheim
Illustrated by Chris Demarest

A Byron Preiss Book

Gareth Stevens Publishing
**MILWAUKEE**

One day a little black crow
spotted a sack of corn seed
lying on the ground.

"Caw, caw!" he crowed.
"Just what we need—
a sack of seed!"

So the little black crow
flew back to the farm.

"Caw, caw!" he crowed.
"Look what I found just lying around.
Who will help me plant
these seeds in the ground?"

"Not now," mooed Cow.

"I'm asleep," baaed the Sheep.

"Oh," cawed Crow. "Then I will do it
ALL BY MYSELF."

Soon the sprouts were tall and green, but weeds were growing in between.

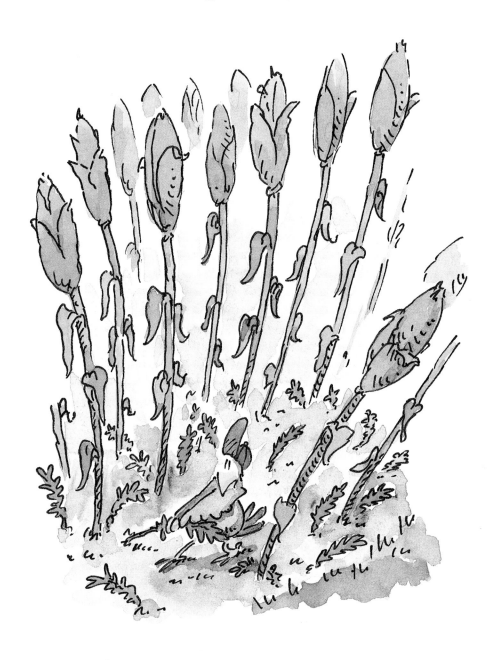

"Who will help me pull the weeds?"

"Nix, nix!" peeped the Chicks.

"I'm asleep," baaed the Sheep.

"Not now," mooed Cow.

"Oh," cawed Crow. "Then I will do it ALL BY MYSELF."

The rows of corn grew tall and thick.
Soon, fat green ears were ready to pick.

"Who will help me pick the corn?"

"Why me?" brayed Donkey.

"Nix, nix!" peeped the Chicks.

"I'm asleep,"
baaed the Sheep.

"Not now,"
mooed Cow.

"Oh," cawed Crow. "Then I will do it
ALL BY MYSELF."

Crow picked the ears one by one,
and late that night his work was done.

"Who will help me shuck the corn?"

"Don't be funny,"
squealed the Bunny.

"Why me?"
brayed Donkey.

"Nix, nix!" peeped the Chicks.

18

"I'm asleep," baaed the Sheep.

"Not now," mooed Cow.

"Oh," cawed Crow. "Then I will do it ALL BY MYSELF."

Now all that corn was still on the cob, and taking it off was a big, big job.

"Who will help me shell the corn?"

"Not my job,"
grunted Hog.

"Don't be funny,"
squealed the Bunny.

"Why me?"
brayed Donkey.

"Nix, nix!"
peeped the Chicks.

"I'm asleep,"
baaed the Sheep.

"Not now," mooed Cow.

"Oh," cawed Crow. "Then I will do it
ALL BY MYSELF."

Then Crow put the corn into a pot.
"What we need," he said,
"is a fire that's hot.

Who will help me gather wood?"

"I can't do that," meowed the Cat.

"Not my job," grunted Hog.
"Don't be funny," squealed the Bunny.
"Why me?" brayed Donkey.
"Nix, nix!" peeped the Chicks.
"I'm asleep," baaed the Sheep.
"Not now," mooed Cow.

"Oh," cawed Crow. "Then I will do it
ALL BY MYSELF."

Soon the wood was burning hot, and
the little black crow put a top on the pot.

"Who will help me shake the pot?"

"I don't dare!" whinnied Mare.

"I can't do that," meowed the Cat.
"Not my job," grunted Hog.
"Don't be funny," squealed the Bunny.
"Why me?" brayed Donkey.
"Nix, nix!" peeped the Chicks.
"I'm asleep," baaed the Sheep.
"Not now," mooed Cow.

"Oh," cawed Crow. "Then I will do it ALL BY MYSELF."

So the little black crow
shook the corn in the pot. . . .
He shook it and shook it
til the pot got hot. . . .

And suddenly,
inside that pot,
the corn got hot
and would not stop.
It just kept going. . .

27

"Where's my share?" whinnied Mare.
"I'll take that!" meowed the Cat.
"That's my job," grunted Hog.
"Yummy, yummy,"
squealed the Bunny.
"For me! For me!" brayed Donkey.
"First licks," peeped the Chicks.
"Let's eat," baaed the Sheep.
"Oh, wow!" mooed Cow.

"No, no!" cawed Crow.
"I planted the seeds.
I pulled the weeds.
When the corn was tall,
I picked it all.
I shucked it, shelled it,
and built the fire.
I shook the pot
til it got hot.
And now I'll eat
this nice, hot popcorn. . .

ALL BY MYSELF."